This Book Belongs To:

Dedication

A big thank you to my family: Denis, Emery, and Leonardo.

Hurray, I get to be in a book!

Thank you to my art instructors,

John Hrehov, Chris Ganz, and Patrick Nerad. — Natalie

Thank you, Mom and Dad. Love you, Leo. — Emery

Push, that's better.

My Mom was making a special pizza

for our Halloween dinner.

You have to start the pizza dough early

in the day to let it rise and double in size.

While we were waiting, something strange happened.

We noticed it was moving.

The dough came alive!

It was growing and rapidly changing.

I threw an onion at it, but it kept coming.

Mom and I tossed green peppers at the monster.

It ate one mid-air.

We slung pepperoni at the dough beast,

but it kept creeping across the counter.

Mom hurled a mozzarella cheese ball at the monstrous dough, but it continue to creep across the counter.

The monster was almost to us.

We were terrified!

It looked so hungry and determined.

Mom dashed cornmeal in an attempt to blind it,

but that didn't work.

I shut the door before it could escape.

We both looked through the oven glass as it began to cook hoping that was the end of it.

When we couldn't resist the delicious smells coming from the oven any longer, we opened the door.

It was big enough to feed the whole family.

The End

Or is it?

Handmade Pizza Dough

2 cups all-purpose flour   500 mL
1 ½ teaspoon quick-rising instant dry yeast 7mL
¾ teaspoon salt   4mL
¾ cup warm water   175 mL
2 teaspoon olive oil   10mL

In large ceramic bowl, combine flour, yeast and salt.
With wooden spoon, gradually stir in water and
oil until dough forms, using hands if necessary.
Turn out onto lightly floured surface,
knead for 8 minutes or until smooth and elastic.

Put dough back in large bowl to rest for 15 to 30 minutes.
Cover the top of bowl with cloth or plastic wrap.

Dust a generous amount of flour onto countertop,
then roll out one 12 inch (30 cm) pizza base or
two 8 inch (20 cm) personal pizza base.

Oven should be preheated at 475 degrees.
Use pizza stone if you have one.

Dust your peel or pizza pan with cornstarch and
cook the dough for 3 to 4 minutes in oven.

Take out pizza dough and add sauce, and toppings.

Cook pizza until you see the mozzarella cheese
start to foam and change. The more toppings on the pizza,
the longer cooking time in the oven.

About the Authors

Emery was six years old when she co-wrote with her mother, Natalie, "The Adventures of Emery: Pizza Monster". In Kindergarten, Emery found her love of writing in Young Author Writing Contest. Shortly after, the duo started to write stories together about Emery's amazing escapades. Natalie has a Masters in Fine Arts and is happy to be putting her day dreams onto paper.

Copyright © 2023 by Natalie Benetti. All rights reserved.

No part of this publication may be reproduced, stored in a retrieval system, or transmitted in any form or by any means, electronic, mechanical,photocopying, recording, or otherwise, without permission of publisher except in the case of brief quotations embodied incritical articles or reviews. For information regarding permission, email publisher at benettinatalie@gmail.com.

ISBN PaperBack: 979-8-9883430-2-8
Library of Congress Control Number: 2023910866
Written by Natalie Benetti and Emery Benetti
Illustrations by Natalie Benetti.

The artwork for this book was created using multimedia. Medias such as watercolor, craftpaper, alcohol ink were used.

First Edition: September 2023

Made in the USA
Middletown, DE
11 September 2023

37829518R00020